I0771594

Gnashing Teeth Publishing
242 East Main Street
Norman AR 71960

Printed in the United States of America

ISBN 979-8-9898345-0-1

Library of Congress Control Number: 2024930452

Poetry, Science Fiction Poetry

Gnashing Teeth Publishing First Edition

PRAISE FOR *SURREALIA*

Surrealia is a love letter and a dirge. It's an ode to a personified place that rustles and sways. It's playful and arty—an architecturally-exquisite assemblage that poises long and short poems segmented into parts.

Eugen Bacon, British Fantasy Award winner, Philip K. Dick Award Nominee and twice World Fantasy Award finalist

Sentience and sapience are spun into eclectic entities by that strange attractor, *Surrealia*. From the Quantum Sea to walking houses, and amidst one man's struggle against a cold, pragmatic empire, Miguel Mitchell's poetic epic takes us on a playful and poignant journey through a world where everything is alive and crackling with poetry.

Come to *Surrealia*: You'll see nothing the same way—ever again.

Bryant O'Hara, author of The *Ghettobirds*

The ending is a crescendo and so unexpected that it won't be discussed here for fear of spoiling it. For this reader it raised gooseflesh. Pulling so many disparate threads together into such a powerful climactic scene is a tour de force.

Overall this book is a full creative universe that someone else might have turned into a thirty book series. In other words, readers should be prepared for a density of idea, creation, detail, and plot twists that may be disorienting in the best way. This is chewy, spicy, and transporting. The destination is partly up to you.

Herb Kauderer

Mitchell has told in verse the old story of resistance against oppression. It's an old story, because it crops up again and again in the real world. Some of the poems in the book are more surreal than others;... However, the collection as a whole is a beautiful and surreal landscape of, perhaps, our own future.

David C. Kopaska-Merkel

A riveting read that will resonate especially with readers interested in post-apocalyptic and quirky science fiction poetry, *Surrealia* by Miguel O. Mitchell is original, thought-provoking, and yet playful, gently leavened by humor and a companionable voice.

Please welcome the debut collection of an ingenious bard ready to disrupt your quietude with a seemingly endless supply of "phantasmal entities." This is a fascinating page-turner of provocative verses and surreal randomness.

Elgin Award winner, LindaAnn LoSchiavo, *Apprenticed to the Night* and *Always Haunted: Hallowe'en Poems*

SURREALIA
by
Miguel O. Mitchell

Table of Contents

FOREWARD

Line by line Surrealia slides us into a stunning psychedelic otherness of alien planet experience. We are reminded of the ways in which variants can perturb and frighten, and dismay or dazzle in this sensory laden verse full of color, sound and sight.

Laced with sly humor, the poems all serve an arc, an unfolding multi-variate narrative, which is experienced in the variety of poetic forms used to convey us through archaic and limiting dualities: love and war, endings and beginnings, arrivals and departures, that are constantly challenged and shed.

Miguel O. Mitchell employs, explodes every sense as we stagger stumble, travel, and encounter this unknown land that offers both beauty and searing, startling experience from its inception through its peregrinating, mind -expanding conceptions.

I love "sentient clouds" that leave one dripping with insight as the poet plays games with perception, the eigenstates, observer-elected realities. We are led to inhabit an alien otherness where the planet is sentient, self-protective, procreative and multidimensional.

It's a singular delight to experience such a compelling page turner about a future evolution that resonates with our now – for the end of all our exploring will be to arrive where we started and be free.

Years ago I read a story where human voyagers by the intake of air, never mind food might be rendered high in a profoundly altered state, such as that supplied by an advanced hallucinogenic. I'm reminded to of how aliens got drunk on sour milk on TV series and how a recent anime shows what may perhaps be its usual bio mechanics on an alien planet is disturbingly, distractingly, frighteningly odd.

We humans have just begun to pierce how our neighbors perceive the light spectrum that we cannot and the sound that we cannot. Our "dull" ocean depths are multihued, radiant, and redolent with hue.

We are just beginning to question rankism and hierarchy, our rigid adherences to choice suppressing orthodoxies, oppressive linear orientations. Surrealia urges us toward surrender and affirmation, doing the wondrous work of the engaged speculative to imagine another glorious, better way to be.

Thank you, Miguel, for this journey into a beyond that goes within, turns us inside out, reinvigorates and offers hope and joy.

It's a wow!

Akua Lezli Hope, Elgin and Rhysling Award winning speculative poet and an SFPA Grandmaster

1.
few rules apply on Surrealia
but one thing is certain
no spacesuits allowed
ballistic-proof starship armor
is a meal swallowed by the winds
chunks dispersed like spider silk
a risk-reward exchange
exposure entry fee

the first ten days outside i raged with fever
nurse phantoms attended me
a misty form shoved a hand in my mouth
condensing into cooling water
another massaged my head
with a chilly fogbank

once the heat subsided
my helpers dissipated
but slowly enough
to leave a small rainbow

2.
walkabout
after a hundred or so kilometers
the brush became grassland

in the daytime
a hip deep sea
waving green reeds with tiny pink flower tops
warm to the touch
sighing with photonic pleasure

at night
bioluminescent splendor
a glowing crimson ocean
rippling waves
with groans of discontent

then the night bees came
a black shrieking horde
hooding the lamps of the double moons

they surged around me
a stone in a raging river
no stings or bites
just a thousand dismissals
not flower
                not flower
                        not flower

3.
the farmers
skinny metallic gold hued bipeds
clad in variegated rings
hatchet heads downward *thunk*
blue soil quivers

warm purple geysers spray
then arterial pulsations
seep glug seep glug seep
hand-sized seeds are buried
in violet-edged wounds

in a blink
full growth attained
an *n*-dimensional crystalline tree
sprawling fractal majesty

branches slip dip spiral
poke into other universes

transparent leaves collect moisture
rain from other realities

i don't sleep here
dreams tend to manifest

4.
my physics colleague hated Surrealia
mountain mirages casting no shadows
floating above an orange frothing ocean
ginger mockery of an azure sky
phantasmal entities
multiverse spanning constructs
too much to explain
nothing to nurture
smug
        intellectual
                    superiority
he felt small here
i said *that's just reality*
his reply
derogatory string theory

5.
the flying range
beings leapt from mountain peaks
over valleys filled with glass shard teeth
wingless but hopeful
briefly falling from uncertainty
then buoyed up by diamagnetic miracles
repulsive love for free-willed water bags
selecting quantum states with abandon
swooping
            soaring
                      diving
up and down the eigenstates
observer selected realities
respect for the random
that is Surrealia

6.
puffy sentient clouds
grayish green and ominous
hover and chortle

mind-pounding thunder
concrete staleness shattered
a neural reset

lightning flashes above
zap dormant synapses
ion currents flood

clarity amidst the gloom
the rain soaks me with ideas
i drip with insight

7.
my physicist friend is leaving
a dead world beckons
advanced tech
from alien ghosts

i ask
will we be any richer
when we have all the gold?
he sneers
one day you'll understand
the value
             of soulless
                         technocracy
at that point
he seems to
disappear

i smile
he has so much to learn

8.
riding on the back of a concept
fleshed out from dream matter
hurtling six-legged through visions
soil flung behind
new
        worlds
                    born

its bifurcated head
swaying tasting
adjacent realities
'til a hard stop
flings me off
into a field of laughing Buddhas
i am so delighted
not sure if i can find my body

9.
warbling whistle welcome
from Phew-Phaw-Phew
a fellow traveler
their birdsong greeting conflicts
with their gray hooded cobra appearance
serpentine and legless
cloaked in a lightless robe
looming above me by a foot
the shadow of scaly sharp-toothed death
but that's just my hindbrain squawking

i whistle back in style
four golden slitted eyes
wide, oval, and moist
slow blink in appreciation

walking and slithering
side by side
we head for the tournament
we're partners at free will
the game
where everybody wins

in the game of free will
there are four players
and there are infinite players
we use a deck of cards
and we do not play with cards
each player reveals
in undetermined sequence
their card/not-card
vision
        possibility
                        action
influenced by the game
some players
change form
that is, of course, ridiculous

form being
an illusion
Phew–Phaw–Phew plays
cosmic wheel
my turn
we switch perspectives
worldview bonus +10
blessed otherness

10.
an interstellar armada in orbit
bristling with death worship
orgiastic oblivion
the promise of
deeply penetrating
coherent nihilism

achieving their plateau
their photon seeds spray
and Surrealia responds
dropping scented flower petals
from the stratosphere

she is an amused partner
but wholly unsatisfied

understandably embarrassed
the armada tries to flee
but a gentle clasp of force
a spacetime sheathed glove
pulls them to her breast
they swoon in the reimagining
of their existence

11.
i cross into the dim valley
the low crimson light a balm
perpetual dusk loved by red dwarf kin

black grassy huts meander
sentient homes on the move
striding a story-tall
bark-sheathed legs and three-toed feet
sometimes used as hands

out of the grass poke false oval heads
two for courtesy
glowing in greeting
their word name is Violet Red Shimmer
a longtime friend

i climb up the resting hut as they crouch
and the pulsating headlights message "enter"
as they slip back inside

i leave my boots and socks outside
always walk barefoot inside a hut
their home is their body
the rug is their tongue

four false heads in total
fix meaningless expressions
misdirect lunch for ancient predators
replaceable
heart and mind
secure within
a blood-warmed sanctuary

the steamy living room
curls its tongue for me to sit on
an honor

using my weak photonic ability

i flicker
what did you think of the flower petals?
the heads illuminate playfully
they taste like hubris
          with a hint
                    of desperation
we both flash erratically in laughter

12.
every visitor to Surrealia
gets a one-and-infinite doorway
meeting myself
multiplied manyfold
martyrs miscreants malefactors
monikered Max or Maxwell or Maximillian
hold a support group on Surrealia
the living fifteen so far
dead Maxes use other doorways
but we don't have invitations

Max-1096 raises his hand
tells us his tale of being born
in the wrong body
on a barely interplanetary earth
his parents wanting a Misty
we chorus "you are Max"
eliciting a shy smile
hand absently rubbing
shirt-covered binder
Max-1096 likes this dream
not being scorned
or beaten
there's a party at Zane's
but after
the street has wolves

body switch i suggest
Max-1096 to 511
rest and be whole
I'll bear the brunt tonight

Surrealia thinks it's fun
wicked little djinn
the former Max-1096 shouts with joy
hugs himself/myself
but in his body
damn that binder is tight

another wish invoked
the other Maxes gasp
"why are you holding a neural disrupter?" Max-57 asks
the one-and-infinite doorway appears behind me
"it's for the after party"
and i step through

13.
i want to swim in the Quantum Sea
sign on the beach says
beware of tunneling

heck with it
i body surf
on waves of duality
wiping out
and hanging ten
simultaneously

floating on twinkling
transient
matter
wetness state = 1
i wave at less of myself
still sitting on the sand

14.
the monster show
one of Surrealia's best events
my shackles have padding
comfort being key
when you walk naked in shame
dragged by the huge hounds
of superiority
my people fed them well

the other species boo
throw mud of oppression at me
quite the sting
remind me how horrible i was/am/will be

after the pantomime
we party
                wait
                            not what you expected?

15.
i lie in the violet forest
neath a parliament of trees
leaves shaped like four-fingered hands
clap in approbation
as they sway and rustle
against the perfumed wind

i know that scent
it's called letting go

16.
hop hop hop
the microstars sizzle puddles
superdense gas babies
giddy with fusion
i bend to watch
due to the gravity of the situation

17.
i go spelunking
Surrealia style
free falling
ropes are for the uninvited

the cavern is bigger
than my imagination
its depths make me somber
i smell omniprescence

suddenly insensate
i wonder
have i reached the bottom?
or the top?

as the Quantum Sea foam
births me like Venus upon the twinkling shore

inhaling awareness makes me cry
face pressed to her nanite bosom
Surrealia sings me to sleep

18.
here they come the marching metal
nano ferro magnet glee

pumped up with that valence band width
current surging amperes free

flailing screeching crashing circus
cymbal arms do smack and spin

shiny rods arc flash and tumble
slip betwixt and leap within

snap now flowing silver chalice
conductive blood a gleaming pool

19.
elephantine wet eyes float lazily in a broken sky
a four-color-theorem patchwork
paper mâché clouds drift by on fire
as thunder rumbles in our brains
soft
        present
                        enough
occasional tears rain down
we catch them on our tongues
they taste just like the view

20.
eastern continental preserve
a chittermink named Teep-Teep
no taller than my knee
like a talking squirrel
with a lot on their mind
leads me by the hand
and narrates

Max, look at the mirrorlopes
racing across the orange spongefield
blinding flashes from metallic hides
steel whip tails snapping behind them
blue-white sparking joy

don't stare at the reflections
you might see unwanted truths

and now we enter the Jumble
see it ahead
it expects us to hold the beat
as we glide
inside
follow my paw rhythm
ba paw ba, paw paw
bapaw bapaw bapawpaw
bababa, paw paw
bapaw bapaw bapawpaw

in the non-distance
exploding from the soil
bubbleacious Sylph
they are living to boil

foaming skin ruptures
existence is in motion
spheroplastic swells
effervescent devotion

next see the Zinkla
blue shifting spinning platters
consume rocks and stones
leaving gemstones in shatters

last spy the Fel Yorg
like giants in old earth tales
voices boom with pride
singing wonder with bass wails

now this tour's done Max
i hope you return often
for the Jumble path
reason's edges will soften

i waved farewell to Teep–Teep
as they transformed
from a furry companion
to a willowy phantasm
to
what was i talking about?

THE MUSEUM TOUR

21. The Anharmonic Museum – Exterior

the tower writhes
a cloud-piercing behemoth
upper sections twist haphazardly
right-handed helix
left-handed helix
color shifts from red to ultraviolet
my emotions dance across their own spectrum

rocky midsection expands like bellows
the lungs of Prometheus
the exhalation tickles my feet
ground swell fascination

the doorway S curves and slides
soft golden bricks frame the edges
surface twinkling and gel wriggling
my sinusoidal leap gains me entrance

22. The Anharmonic Museum – Exhibit #1

fire sculpture of the Shrroar
fueled by love and spite
a burning bush without roots or a god

take some warmth
but pay it forward

interactive play sand, yes walk on it, squish it between your lower extremities if you have them, do not eat because the sand parasite has no further need for hosts, thank you, it has grown beyond dependency but is wistful, use your imagination to build castles, no, not your hands, that's very intimate don't you think, we should get to know each other first, there you go, such a lovely pedestrian construction with turrets and a moat, i see that you took the word castle literally, let's try again, ah parallel floating square layers of impulsive whims rotating in opposite directions sandwiching thick slabs of neglect, nicely done and so personally insightful

24. The Anharmonic Museum – Exhibit #3

wooden dresser with a top and a bottom but no sides
all drawers are invisible but wish to be seen
their contents refuse to be useful

look, you found a penny
that weighs a pound
neutron matter money
that doesn't matter at all

pull on this spot
a drawer appears
made of flesh
inside an eye winks at you
you push it back
slightly embarrassed

25. Call From My Brother

my neuroimplant informs me
my brother Aaron is calling
a spacetime warp dose of misery
i answer anyway
Aaron bellows
hey Max, you refreshed yet?
centered
          enlightened
                 transcendent
                        full of shit
yet?
i respond
still working mines on that planet?
our family legacy
sentients turned into drug-fueled zombies
digging ore for every precious score
we slave descendants now slavemasters
cuz if so brother
i'll keep my shit
one day you may realize
you're swimming in it

my brother disconnects
no surprise
same thing he did
when his conscience called

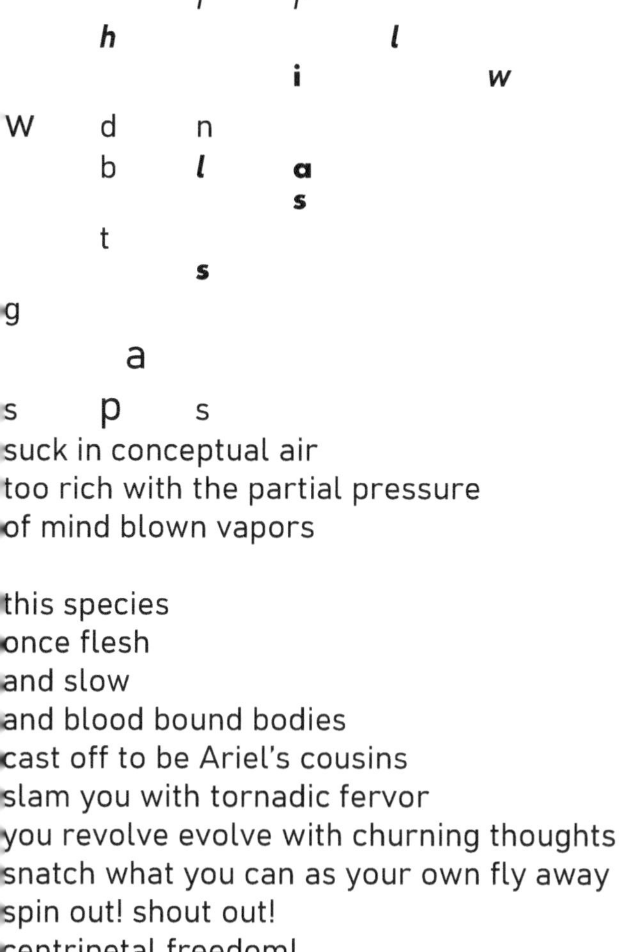

suck in conceptual air
too rich with the partial pressure
of mind blown vapors

this species
once flesh
and slow
and blood bound bodies
cast off to be Ariel's cousins
slam you with tornadic fervor
you revolve evolve with churning thoughts
snatch what you can as your own fly away
spin out! shout out!
centripetal freedom!
release!
your body drops to the floor
pant and pant
crying from the loss
burdened again by this prison
limbs and solidity
sweet memory dissipates
o elemental oneness!
o gaseoussss
freeeee
gone

27. The Anharmonic Museum – Exhibit #5

an eight-limbed Vlip
Glacial Elegance their ex-military name
a reflection of idleness prized in retirement
short crimson hairs and chartreuse skin
head and body stalk-like
four legs folded on a seat
a giant, gray fossilized mushroom
two pairs of arms lie limp by their sides
two pairs of fur-covered eyelids closed
central eating probiscis pinched and chest laden
glossy crimson beak sealed
their immobility induces me to sit on the floor
to just enjoy each breath

a holographic display begins
various species in time-slowed attacks
blades moving through gelatinous air
then a startling motion
the beak pops open
a villanelle begins

now-one-one-thousand-two-one-thousand merged
the youthful Vlip their brains predict and spy
foresight that lasts til blessed old age purged

in hand-to-hand combat are Vlip kids urged
'gainst species beaten by their time slip sly
now-one-one-thousand-two-one-thousand merged

they learn to kill and keep concerns submerged
just know those future moves and battle cry
foresight that lasts til blessed old age purged

as martial skills soon bore and wonder surged
about the peoples cultures worlds on high
now-one-one-thousand-two-one-thousand merged

no more the whips with which races were scourged
put up their tools of death and now know why
foresight that lasts til blessed old age purged

they barely move at home their lives diverged
in stillness gone the future-seeing eye
now-one-one-thousand-two-one-thousand merged
foresight that lasts til blessed old age purged

28. Sending a Present to My Brother

a box of crystalline spiders
they look like inert jewels
that's what i'm sending my brother Aaron
my brother who rejects our black ancestor's torments
who thinks free market has meaning
but free will does not
a billion dopamine-surged brains
his chemically harnessed rockhounds
clawing ore to fill his pockets
breaking limbs to eke out that last day's quota
anything to avoid withdrawal
i joined the interstellar expeditionary forces to escape
but i carry my family's atrocity in my head
so, Aaron, enjoy the spiders
they are only active at night
so, while you sleep
out will emerge the vanguards
of the holy church
of abolitionism
an obscure but zealous faith
powered with mind-healing anti-venom
replicating exponentially with each enlightened convert
you are going to have an interesting time
say hello to the archbishop for me

29. The Anharmonic Museum – Exhibit #6

darkness
let it embrace
cold haunts
freeze time itself
one breath
that holds a universe
endless

a crowded room of sentients **exit**
a door for each old just like the **museum**
portal precise pathway perceived **but**
uncertainties still to final form **donate**
imperceptible the loss of fleshy **pieces**
sympathetic books of cells tell stories **of**
the tales exquisite unique you **yourself**
enshrined in proper pageantry thus **for**
the nascent patron fed with something **new**
as chaos reigns its teaching style **exhibits**

Max's Journey

31. Utilitaria

o shuttle bay awaits me that i dread
the faithless queen collects her drones to serve
Utilitaria her heartless name
to crush us worthless creatures task by task
and sterilize our minds that birth free will
we puppets fancy strings enchanted us
we puppets fancy strings enchanted us
and sterilize our minds that birth free will
to crush us worthless creatures task by task
Utilitaria her heartless name
the faithless queen collects her drones to serve
o shuttle bay awaits me that i dread

32. Orchard Stroll

i walk midst pregnant trees
their swollen bounty freely offered
taste my nectar say the whispers
red fruit for rich thoughts
green for growth
violet for victims
standing 'neath a low bough
i gorge on purple devastation
the juice of despair
dripping screams down my chin

my body is skeletal
pampered flesh consumed
to feed lost innocence

i regurgitate the seeds
they glow with an inner light
digging with my hands nearby
i plant hope
it always sprouts tall and improbable
where you least expect it

33. The Return of the Physicist

an auspicious day
my physicist friend returned
sitting on a particle dune
looking out at the Quantum Sea

"they cut my strings," he said
his eyes held galaxies
as the wind blew seaward
his body particulated
a disintegrating sand castle
"godhood is relaxing"
the fleeting dust mouth muttered

he no longer belonged to the queen
ruthless practicality a forbidden eigenstate
i danced my gratitude

34. Poem Recited by a Winged Brown Stick Insect on My Shoulder before It Flew Off

dis zizz vee zow wee low mo mo
muh mo keh low hey hey
in dezvir mahk kreh fu fu tor
free teema schirr cro may

na fen zee qua dey quis ru ru
la ru zee quis kay kay
ilf yakwa choat pah tu tu for
see vora beer tro fay

35. Garden of Echoes

the yellow fan
accordions out with the rising sun
metronome-like waving spreads its fluffy pollen
breathe in the history

grasping for eternity in space
found decency too slippery
they left a pretty graveyard
#
the orange jet sprayer
swollen bulb
building building
tight at the seams
begging for release
a flyby insect oh
triggers that little death
the pollen-coated recipient
an unrequited paramour
your face will serve as well
for plant bukkake

the sticky seeds bear a honeyed tale
furry conquerors black and silky
worlds to shape as warped reflections
ignoring what they shatter
a virus born in the lungs of the oppressed
slaughtered these ursine overlords faster than plasma fire
the infected slaves now masters
have kept their homes up nicely
traces of the previous owners
carted off with the other trash
#
the black needle launcher
spits lances at passing creatures
flesh is as good as soil
but you don't want to wake up as a bush
so, unpluck these shards but please plant them

they balk at being disrespected

the toxin-borne story of the spike unfolds
gleaming towers of diamond lattice
cloud-wrapped temples of gold and platinum
amidst the swept streets of whitest stone

the wraiths wander
existential oscillations
oblivion to tenuous
trying to remember
we wove the pattern
races bent to our will
a stable of weak-minded chattel
neural chained by our telepathy
but there was this place/not-place
foolish ants hiding there
from our righteous foot
we tried to stomp
to stomp
to
we wove the pattern...

Surrealia smiles in my mind
this is her favorite acquisition

36. Letter From Home

squawking dissonance in my head
distraction makes me lose the match
my mental arm-wrestling with Max-478
just one strenuous cranial surge
and they would have liked chocolate
instead, i disgustingly fancy beets

here's the neural missive in summary:
you broke the law sending crystal spiders that freed a chemically
enslaved populace
your home world is quarantined to keep those spiders from
spreading the misery of free will
take that hated shuttle
turn yourself over to interstellar expeditionary force command aka
asshole central
you will be arrested, tried, convicted, and paraded around the galaxy
as an object lesson to others even thinking about, well, thinking
your telovirus has been remotely activated, thus you have two solar
days to comply before your chromosomes are snipped done to nubs,
and your cells decide to take a dirt nap
that is all

Max-478 asks me why i'm crying
i tell them i've decided to die on Surrealia
and i'm afraid that oblivion might taste like beets
they pat me on the shoulder
there, there, they say
on Surrealia
oblivion surely tastes like
everything

37. Death Day

my last sunrise
shining through my viewport
illuminating a forest
of zigzag trees

oblivion is a comfort
compared to neural realignment
death of personality
whatever's on the menu
but losing Surrealia
is still a dagger to my heart

didn't believe it could get worse
 til a new neural missive screeched
thinking about just dying?
well, your home world is still alive
protected from xenophobic scum
by a radiant queen
unless she is sadly preoccupied

as an object lesson for disobedience
planetary genocide by proxy
would pay the bill
if it comes due
that is all

'm suddenly under a building
a tower made from billions of lives
crushing my resolve

 trudge toward the despised shuttle
my limbs heavy as blocks of ice
all feeling numbed by subzero reality

38. Surrealia Revealed

closer closer i come my heart doth crack
i near the ship that sends me to my doom
the pav-ed road though silver now seems black
and flowers on both sides now smell of gloom

then all before me fades as in a dream
and on a platform midst a spectral storm
a chaos beauty shifting layered gleam
Surrealia my love has taken form

stay here my darling Max be one with me
your life will flourish when the sun doth sink
that virus imp purged by the Quantum Sea
no weapon here will last more than a blink
astonished by her gift i tell her true
the scheming queen still has an ace to play
if death i chose the bill would still come due
and my home world be shattered if i stay

Surrealia laughs swirling twinkling stars
so be my envoy now and bear my will
return to judgement stayed no prison bars
your home world through my power peace will fill

i swear to her my oath and feel so light
she wraps her essence 'round me through me vast
joined now such concepts complex and so bright
but strangely love in all worlds meant to last

the road appears again but now doth shine
the flowers flanking me a fragrant cheer
my head held high i march up the incline
into the shuttle facing the guards sneer

they try to bind me but all chains dissolve
force fields to cage do warp before they fail
i sit down quietly my thoughts revolve
their fear grows large but no threats i assail

39. Return to IEF Command

the shuttle docks in IEF command
crisp snap-tos as rod-like rigidity
hails moral-gray stupidity
the brass have come to see this strange bird
foolishly thinking its wings aren't clipped

i stand but do not salute
one of death's disciples barks
Show some respect! You are still an IEF soldier!
i smile and explain
that was Max in another iteration
my quantum states no longer allow
obsequious transitions
i, Max, represent Surrealia
tell Utilitaria i'm no longer
her bitch

alarms blare
a chaos-driven starship
sighs into blurry existence
that's my ride i exclaim
and with a wink
i wink out
reappearing in a tie-dyed chair
a variegated command console
flesh warm with organic contours
this living vessel embraces me
then my brain floods
such wondrous memory
for Teep-Teep is the pilot
i forgot about you!
Teep-Teep squeaks
it wasn't time for you to remember

the ship makes a purring sound
quite satisfied with herself
as we move away from the space station

energy blasts and explosions rock us
looking out the viewport
i see the weapons' fire
birthed ephemeral space creatures
the plasma guns are like teats
the babes suck energy milk from
Teep-Teep takes us to my home world
i just shake from laughter

40. Max Returns to His Home World

our ship names herself La Nueva Forma
the new way in Old Earth Spanish
liking how the sounds tickle her awareness
syllables round and rich
passionate and profound

she folds spacetime in some exotic manner
disintegrating distance
as we now orbit my home world
she telechats with me and Teep-Teep
o this is feeling the warmth of a star
life below in all its majesty
cosmic connected commentary
dynamic disequilibrium defined

i ask her where she came from
Surrealia birthed me, she says
as she did Teep-Teep
we are chaos kin
none look alike

time to see what i wrought
in a flash i stand before Aaron
who lunges for my throat
his brotherly greeting
you've destroyed our legacy, he screams
as he tightens on flesh made stone
like Aaron's heart

gently removing his hands, i say
mining despair is not a legacy worth keeping
there were further depths to plumb, he cries
i nod
there always are
his ship of arrogance had crashed and sunk
clothes unkempt, skin reeking of cerebralock
the master himself enslaved

by a siren song that promised love
on a sea of dopamine-inducing waves
that turn to screeching harpies claws rending
when shallow are the narcotic pools

robot servants arrive
they fawn and pamper my wretched brother
echo chambers for deluded victimization
soothing lies as balms for moral turpitude

annoying humming force field
blocks the righteous fury
of an unchained populace

i step outside and channel
Surrealia's gift
Snap!
suddenly so quiet
you can hear a sin drop

there is a flood arriving
to cleanse the land
cerulean-shelled free Intaki
antennae twitching
forelimbs bristling with weapons

though i will mourn my brother
lost long ago
this is the Intaki's world again
and sometimes
for a wound to heal
the pus must be let out

41. Max Greets the Archbishop of the Crystal Spiders

wandering and numb
groundswell sunburst behind me
the light of new beginnings
the deafening roar of rage
howls heat my back
from explosive
family
annihilation
but has no warmth

tap tap on my foot
a crystal spider emissary
i follow it like a zombie
but sadly i still breathe

space-time shift
i stand before the archbishop
his crystalline magnificence looms
an eight-legged titan sparkling with facets
growth fed by a billion believers
freedom is a nourishing stew

six emerald-like hexagonal eyes, hard as stone
somehow gaze down on me softly
welcome, Max
 have felt your vibrations
on the web of existence
but here you are on thick strands
easier to oscillate to this place

thank you for saving the Intaki i say
the archbishop's laughter is the tinkling of glass chimes
saving is for missionaries
dominating the will of others
anathema to our beliefs
we simply heal wounds in the mind
break neuropathway shackles

savoring the instant choices blossom
a garden of possibilities
then walk away

what will your people do now that you are stuck here?
enjoy our existence
give advice when asked
watch the unfolding
so many lovely petals

one day i will consume my last photons
my crystal sliding phase will transition
i will know mineral transcendence
a blessed rock of oblivion

but before the end
there is a new age coming
we the crystal spiders
grind our fore plates in anticipation
see you again soon
harbinger

with a question on my lips
i am whisked back to La Nueva Forma
Teep-Teep shakes his head at my puzzled expression

42. The Team Gets to Work

La Nueva Forma flexes
trans-dimensional neck cracking
a fleet of xenophobes attack my world
antimatter missiles launch
their shells coated with a culture of disdain
filled with the lust of genocidal frenzy
they are a quantum singularity of hatred
thus, as a constructive waveform
i propagate them elsewhere

Teep-Teep sends echoes of mirrorlopes
racing down the starship corridors
contingencies fly from minds fleeing
hide reflections cast doubt
the certainty of superiority crumbles
a worldview built on sand

La Nueva Forma contacts the ship minds
eager for intelligent conversation
they ignore orders to launch more attacks
missile bays closed
it's time for the children to shush
adults are speaking

an agreed upon transform
an inverted spacetime pinch
and we are at the xenophobes' homeworld
their missiles fast approaching
they have more than enough time
luckily i'm not a monster yet
the starships give La Nueva Forma
bye-bye cyberkisses
as gamma ray lasers
mop up their kids' mess

43. Royal Decree

interstellar neurotransmission auto-activated:
hear ye, hear ye!
presenting her imperial sublime authority
supreme ruler of the earthcentric dominion of worlds
communicating from the royal gardens
Queen Utilitaria the first!

my subjects
see my pruning shears
i loathe to use
you are such dears

but weeds abound
they fester blight
they must be purged
to bring pure light

Surrealia
it's name a bane
it sickens minds
a moral stain

thus i decree
from this day hence
that world is banned
for your defense

i know it hurts
to lose your fun
vacation spot
from cares to run

but Mother Queen
she knows what's best
bow to my will
i'll do the rest

    -    end transmission

44. The Envoy Returns

returning to Surrealia
cloaked warships in all directions
a sphere of invisible death

so many minds yet to open
spreading a viral message
free will is infectious

Teep-Teep's idea kicks my melancholy in the teeth
jaw-jarring me out of complacency
we orbit Surrealia for a call to action

La Nueva Forma becomes her best selves
three-hundred and eighty-two of them
each is every, every is each
a quantum-entangled gestalt
one for every empire-ravaged world

volunteers board ready for adventure
cultural advisors to explain a grand exchange
their people swapped with cosmic alt-kin
via shipborne multiverse portals

as iterations 1 discover Surrealia
iterations 2 enjoy the novelty
play acting in exchange for self-revelation
learning lines to try an untrodden path

45. The Ruse Discovered

parallel worlds once warred
the carcasses of the fallen buried in the elsewhere
from the unmarked burial plots flowers sprouted
limp blossoms that nod and cry sweet nectar
clenching leaves nearly ripping in distress

imperial gardeners pull out these strange mourners
it hurts every time

fear of more existential conflict led to the inter-hounds
dogs trapped between realities
their phantasmal noses sniffing out the variants
the scent of spies from other universes
triggering howls of despair
take me with you!
save me from this purgatory, this un-life!
unable to eat
but always starving
unable to breathe
but always smelling
unable to rest
but always tired

their pleas are misunderstood
the ones the dogs seek in their agony
potential saviors from the multiverse
die at the hands of their imperial handlers
for the inter-hound is like the fabled fox
leaping at grapes always out of reach

someone had this bright, devastating idea
when a ship from Surrealia appears
have the inter-hounds do a sweep for variants
after all, Surrealia has portal technology
time to mark the wickedness boxes
inter-universe visitations uncovered
check

replacement citizens disintegrated
check
they didn't belong in our reality anyway
is it murder if you were never supposed to exist?
and the originals who returned
they were put to death slowly
for all citizens to see
on forced
brain raping
neurotransmissions
check
Utilitaria explained to the shocked and the outraged
(the latter would of course be monitored)
just pulling weeds from our garden, citizens
nasty weeds filled with unpleasant thoughts
bad thoughts spread like dandelions
and they must be plucked
before their tiny seeds are nurtured
by subversive soil

46. Uprising

Teep-Teep 's voice is too far away
Max has no ears for a kind word
those sounds existed in the past
the present only offers the screams of the tortured
 and the roar of skull-splitting rage

the power of the envoy
to create or destroy
across hundreds of worlds Max sees a future
imperial troops writhe forever
being stabbed and healed
on spikes of living glass shards
Utilitaria visits each of her worlds
as a brightly burning living star
in eternal agony

Surrealia sends a neural breeze
cooling thoughts of fiery devastation
my envoy my love
that was me once
until i retreated into solace
it's so hard to stand back
to let a baby stumble
you want to kiss away all the hurts
but your answer would crown you
king Max the first
king Max the terrible
king Max the destroyer
Teep-Teep 's voice reaches Max
let each person decide
Max taps Surrealia's core
a question rips through space-time
roars down on almost four hundred worlds
where the story of Surrealia is a bittersweet notion
a sanctuary spoken in whispers
tainted by the death of thousands

people with hands and legs
wings and beaks
claws and pseudopods
folks who clash in the streets against the forces of conquest
who bleed in rainbow colors for their common personhoods
who hide their offspring from the ravages of sickened worlds
they all hear it
in the depths of their despair-shredded spirits
they all hear it
what do you want?
and the answer is always the same
Freedom!
Freedom!
Freedom!
and the combined crest of a quantum wave
amplified by a trillion coherent desires
crashes against the forces of Utilitaria
this simple act of accelerated entropy
a little thing really
like when iron rusts
or a mountain crumbles
and the energy weapons
and the planet bombs
and the gas grenades
and the flesh-piercing projectiles
all fail
the people are a sea of change
and the tide has turned
the empire is chased from its own worlds
the greatest blessing?
the silence of the neuro-net
no more pronouncements from a deposed queen
her weeds have revolted
they are the garden now

back on Surrealia
Max and Teep-Teep and La Nueva Forma prepare
billions will visit Surrealia
there is a party about to happen

who knows how long it will last?

let the stars swell with pride
let the planets tremble in their gratitude
let Despair back his bags
and tip his hat farewell
your bizarre notions of free will
they seemed silly compared to puppetry
dancing to my whims
tried and true for aeons
but you beat me fair and square
   world weaver
      paradigm shifter
         teacher of the lost
            disciple of hope
               sister of chaos

Surrealia

Acknowledgements

Surrealia 16. *Star*Line*, vol.46.4, Fall 2023.

I wish to thank the members of the Speculative Poetry Workshop, sponsored by the Baltimore Science Fiction Society, for their encouragement and helpful suggestions. I particularly appreciate the influence of my two poet brothers in musical verse, Bryant O'Hara and Tavair Tapp, who inspired me to let my poems sing. I also thank my wife Laura for always being proud of me and supporting my creativity.

About the Author

Miguel O. Mitchell, PhD (he/him) is a Black speculative poet, SFF author, visual artist, and retired chemist. His poems have appeared in *Amazing Stories*, *Dreams & Nightmares*, *Eye to the Telescope*, *Scarlet Dragonfly Journal*, *Scifaikuest*, *Star*Line*, and the anthology *Year's Best African Speculative Fiction* (2022). He has also published a poetry collection, *Periodic Table of Alien Species (Elements 1-86)* (Barnes & Noble Press, 2021).